First published in the United States in 2023 by Sourcebooks

The illustrations in this book were created in Adobe Photoshop using digital painting and found textures.

Published by Sourcebooks Jabberwocky, an imprint of Sourcebooks Kids
P.O. Box 4410, Naperville, Illinois 60567-4410
(630) 961-3900
sourcebookskids.com

Originally published as *Keys* in 2014 in New Zealand by Huia Publishers.

Cataloging-in-Publication Data is on file with the Library of Congress.

Source of Production: Leo Paper, Heshan City, Guangdong Province, China
Date of Production: November 2022
Run Number: 5028376

Printed and bound in China.
LEO 10 9 8 7 6 5 4 3 2 1

When DADDY Tucks Me In

Words by Sacha Cotter   **Pictures by Josh Morgan**

sourcebooks
jabberwocky

Dad works late. I go to bed
before he arrives home.
Every night I fall fast asleep,
until somewhere deep within
my dreams, I hear a jingle, jangle,
jingle in the lock of our door.

I wake up and throw off my blankets.
Then I race down the hallway shouting, "Dad!"

"What are you doing up?" he growls
as he creeps through the door.

I know he's not mad because he's
smiling from ear to ear and he scoops
me up in his big, hairy arms.

"Come on you, let's tuck you back into bed.

Snug as a bug in a rug," he says

as he folds me up in the blankets and tucks me in tight.

"You're the best tucker-in-er-er
in the whole wide world," I say.

I always want Dad to stay longer with me. I take his
enormous bunch of keys and they clatter in my hands.

There are so many! What are they for?

"Dad."
"Yes, love."

"What's this lumpy, bumpy key for?"

"Why, that's the key
to my Zippenburger.

When I leave for
work, I pop outside
to the garage and
I wiggle this lumpy,
bumpy key into
the ignition.

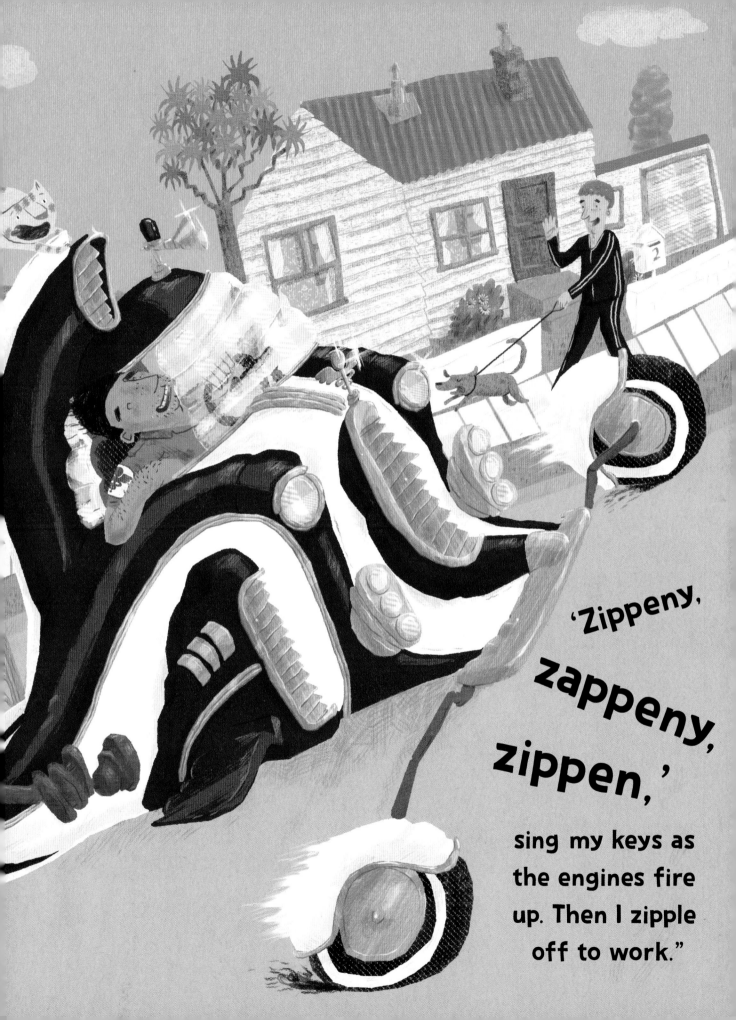

'Zippeny, zappeny, zippen,' sing my keys as the engines fire up. Then I zipple off to work."

"Dad."
"Yes, honey."

"What do you use this eeny, weeny key for?"

"This eeny, weeny key
opens my treasure chest.

It's hidden away at a top-secret location
that's only marked on my pirate's map.
It can be lonely being hidden treasure.
That's why I visit it once a week.

First, I dance a wee jig three times in a clockwise direction. Then I poke the eeny, weeny key in the itty-bitty lock and my keys sing,

'Ooh-argh,
ooh-argh,
ooh-argle.'

My treasure chest creaks open and I polish all the rubies, diamonds, and gold coins until they sparkle."

"And what about this one, Dad?

This curly, curvy one?"

"That curly, curvy key opens a hunky, clunky door at my job. I go there every coffee break. I twist the curly, curvy key in the lock of the hunky, clunky door and my keys sing,

'Wibbily, **wobbily,** wooble.'

Behind the door there's a cookie factory. I sit myself down by a gigantic conveyor belt and I taste-test the freshly baked cookies.

When I find the yummiest, scrummiest cookies, I collect them for my work buddies and we munch them with our coffee."

"What does this rusty key open, Dad?"

"That rusty, old key opens the padlock on a gate to a long-forgotten corral. I squeeze the rusty key into the rusty lock and my keys sing,

'Clinky, clanky, clingle.'

Behind the gate lives Stanley, my woolly mammoth. I ride him round and round the corral to make sure he gets enough exercise.

He's a fussy woolly mammoth. He only eats yellow food. So I take him bananas, pineapples, and bowls of custard sprinkled with lemon drops, all packed in a willow picnic basket."

"What does this long, skinny key do, Dad?"

"That's the key to our work space rocket. On days when we're all extra hungry, I go out the back and I put on my silver spacesuit. My keys sing,

'Shimmery, **shammery,** shoodle,'

as I start up the rocket and shoot into space.

I zoom out past the moon until I'm floating in the stars. Then, in the peaceful blackness, I glide out of the hatch and collect bunches of space noodles. When my arms are overflowing with tasty space noodles, I float back into the rocket and whip back to work before they get cold."

"And what about this key, Dad?"
"This plain, metal key? Why, that's the most important
key of them all. It's my most magical key."

"Wow, what does it open?"

"Every evening I take this plain, metal key, and I turn it in a plain, metal lock, on a plain, wooden door. My keys sing

'Jingle,
jangle,
jingle,'

and I open
the door...
to OUR house.

And do you know what I find waiting for me inside the door?"